Jane Eyre

The Young Collector's
Illustrated Classics

Jane Eyre

By
Charlotte Brontë

Adapted by
Sara Thomson

Illustrated by
Richard Lauter

Cover art by
Richard Lauter

Contents

Chapter 1
My Unhappy Home

It was raining that day, and the cold cut to the bone. I was happy that we did not have to go outside. Usually, Mrs. Reed made us take a walk after dinner. That evening, however, she said we could stay home. So now, her children—Eliza, John, and Georgiana—were in the drawing room, sitting around her by the fireplace.

I walked up to join them and be near the warmth of the fire, but she motioned to me to stay away.

"You've been a bad girl," she said, "and I don't want you near us."

"What have I done?" I asked.

"Don't talk back to me," Mrs. Reed said. "You have an unpleasant manner. You have a bad temper. Little girls should speak pleasantly, always with a smile, or they should keep silent."

I went to another room. It was a small room, with bookcases against the walls and a bay window. I picked up a book, sat on the window seat, and drew the curtain, so I could hide behind it. The book had beautiful pictures of birds in it, but before I could look at more than a few, I heard someone step into the room.

"Boo!" John's voice said. "Miss Longface!"

I'm so glad I closed the curtain, I thought. John is too dumb to guess I'm hiding behind it. Just then, Eliza came into the room, too. Eliza was smart. Eliza guessed right away where I was.

"She's in the window seat," she said to her brother.

I came out from behind the curtain.

"What do you want?" I said.

"Say, 'What do you want, Mr. Reed?'" John said to me. "I want you to come here."

John was fourteen, only four years older than I was. He was tall and fat, and he had a round face with flabby cheeks, dull eyes, and a nasty expression. He would have normally been at boarding school, but his mother had taken him out for a month or two, on account of his "delicate health." The truth was, there was nothing wrong with his health. He felt bad because he overate. He was too lazy to do his schoolwork, so he moped around all day, and stuffed himself with the candy and sweets his mother sent him.

He did not have a loving heart, and he did not show any affection to his mother or his sisters. Me, he hated. He tried to bully me and hurt me all the time. I don't mean just every day. I don't mean just once or twice a day. I mean every chance he had—every time he saw me. I was constantly frightened of him, and there was no one to protect me. His mother pretended she did not see what was going on, and the servants were afraid they would get fired if they took my side.

I walked up to him, as he had commanded me to do. He sneered and pushed me down.

"That's for talking back to Mama," he said. "What were you doing behind the curtain?"

"I was reading."

"Let me see the book."

I went back to the window and brought him the book.

"You have no right to take our books," he said. "You have no right to rummage through our bookshelves. These are our books. This is our house. You have no money, you have no family, and you have no home of your own. You're an orphan. We let you sleep under our roof, we give you food to eat, we give you clothes to wear, but nothing here belongs to you. Go stand in the corner, with your face to the wall."

I obeyed and started to walk away, but before I could take more than two steps, he hurled the book at my back. It was a large, heavy book, and the blow made me fall. As I fell, I hit my head against the edge of a small table. The pain was awful. I had a deep cut on the side of my face, and it bled so much I was scared it wouldn't stop.

"You mean, nasty good-for-nothing—"

"What?" he screamed. "What did you say? Eliza, did you hear her? Did you hear what she called me?"

He grabbed my hair, pulling so hard, I thought it would come out. I kicked, I punched, I scratched—I fought back with all my might.

All at once, Mrs. Reed, Georgiana,

Bessie, who was the nanny, and Abbot, who was one of the servants, burst into the room.

"What's this?" Mrs. Reed said. "What's this!"

"Have you ever seen the like!" Abbot said. "She hit poor Mr. John—she's scratched him!"

"Take her to the red room and lock her in there!" Mrs. Reed said.

"No, please. No!" I begged. But Bessie and Abbot already had a hold of me, and were dragging me up the stairs. I kicked and screamed all the way.

"She's like a mad cat," Bessie said. "Abbot, hold down her arms."

"For shame, Miss Eyre," Abbot said. "Is this a way for a little girl to behave?"

They carried me to the red room and set me down on a stool. The moment their arms were off me, I jumped back up like a spring.

"Sit down, or we'll tie you down," Bessie said. "Abbot, go fetch some rope."

"No! No! Don't tie me down. I don't want to be tied down."

"All right then," Bessie said. "Sit down and sit still."

I sat down on the little stool.

"Make sure you stay there," Bessie said. "Stay there, and think over how bad you've been."

"I'm going to say this to you for your own good, Miss Eyre," Abbot said in a kind voice. "You should try to be nice and pleasant. If you keep displeasing Mrs. Reed, she could throw you out on the street. Who would take care of you then? Remember, you're an orphan and you don't have a penny to your name."

"You should pray to God to forgive you," Bessie said. "You should repent. If you don't repent, a terrible monster is going to come down the chimney and get you."

They left, locking the door.

The red room was the largest and most stately bedroom in the mansion. The floor was covered with red carpet, the windows were draped with red curtains, the bed had a red bedspread on it, and the wallpaper was beige with a pattern of bright red flowers. It was the room in which Mr. Reed had died, and no one had slept in it since. The fireplace had not been lit for years, and the windows were never opened to air out the room. It was damp and cold like a tomb.

I was terrified to be alone in it. It was

very dark. Abbot had left a single candle on the toilet table, and its flame was now flickering weakly. There was a large mirror on the wall. When I looked into it, a white figure with dark eyes like holes looked back. I gave a horrified cry, before I realized I was looking at myself: a thin, pale ten-year-old with a narrow face and large eyes. The dark mirror made me look like a ghoul.

I wished I were pretty. Eliza and Georgiana were pretty and had beautiful, curly blond hair. My hair was dark like my eyes and straight. I was plain, and it was true that I was unpleasant. How could I be pleasant? I was too angry to be pleasant. They were cruel to me, and they were unfair.

If Mr. Reed were still alive, he would make sure I was treated well. I was his sister's child. My mother had married a poor clergyman her parents did not approve of. They disinherited her and would have nothing to do with her at all.

She died when I was born, and my father died from typhoid fever six months later. Mr. Reed took me in. He was a kind man, and he had loved his sister. When he died, he made Mrs. Reed promise him that she would take care of me as if I were her own child. In this very room, standing by this bed, his deathbed, she had promised.

Suddenly, I remembered how it was said that the dead haunt the people who

have done them wrong. Mr. Reed had been wronged by his wife. She had broken the promise she had given him. His ghost is haunting the house, I thought. His ghost comes back in this room, where he died. It's the reason why no one sleeps here. It's the reason they keep it locked.

I knew Mr. Reed had loved me, and that his ghost would be friendly to me, if it appeared, but I was terrified. Good ghost or mean ghost, I did not want to be locked up in a room with one.

Just then, I heard a rattling noise and saw a bright gleam of light shine on the wall. Now, I know it must have been a carriage driving down the road, but at the time I was sure it was Mr. Reed's ghost. I let out a horrified shriek.

Soon I heard footsteps on the stairs. A key turned in the door, and Bessie and Abbot rushed into the room.

"Miss Eyre, what's wrong?" Bessie asked.

"Take me out of here!" I screamed. "Take me out! I saw a ghost."

"She's just saying that," Abbot said.

Mrs. Reed walked into the room. She was in a rage.

"What's all this?" she said. "Bessie, Abbot! What are you doing here? My orders were that Miss Eyre should be locked up in the red room alone."

"She screamed so loud, ma'am," Bessie said.

"Get out!" Mrs. Reed told her. She

turned to me. "You think you can deceive me with your fake screams?" she said. "If there's one thing that's worse than a mean, unpleasant child, it's a child who lies."

"Aunt, please!" I begged. "I'll die if I stay here. Punish me another way! I'll do anything!"

"Silence!" she said. "You'll stay in here till I say you can leave."

She walked out of the room and shut the door.

When I heard the sound of the key turning in the lock, I collapsed on the floor, fainting from fright.

Chapter 2
I Have My Say

The next thing I remember is waking up in my bed. A tall gentleman in dark clothes was bending over my head, peering into my face.

"How are you feeling?" he said.

I told him my head hurt. I touched the spot where the cut was, and felt a bandage.

"Oh, that will get better," he said, giving me a big smile. "I should know, I'm a doctor. Can you tell me what happened?"

"She fell down," Bessie said. She was in the room, standing by the door.

"I was knocked down," I said. "But it wasn't what made me sick. I was locked in the red room, where there's a ghost."

I told the man everything that had happened, just how it had happened.

"How would you like to go to school?" he asked.

I did not know what school would be like, but I said yes, I would. Any place would be better than here, I thought.

The man stared at me thoughtfully, then turned to Bessie. "I'd like to talk to your mistress," he said.

Bessie walked him out, then came back with Abbot. She brought me some cake on a fancy plate, like those she used to serve food for Mrs. Reed and her children.

"Now, you eat this and try to go back to sleep," she said.

How happy I would have been to eat off this beautiful plate, if I were not sick,

if I did not feel so sad! All I wanted to do was cry.

I closed my eyes. They must have thought I had fallen asleep, for I heard Abbot say: "Poor child! I wish I could feel pity for her, but she's so ugly. It's like trying to feel pity for a sick toad."

"I know," Bessie said. "If it were Miss Eliza or Miss Georgiana who were lying in bed with their eyes closed, they'd look like sleeping angels."

"Oh! I dote on Miss Eliza and Miss Georgiana," Abbot said.

Bessie touched my forehead softly with her hand.

"Poor Miss Jane," she said. "I do care for her. But she's too stubborn for her own good."

They left. After a while, I fell asleep.

It took just a few days for my body to heal. But the damage to my soul, dear reader—that, to this day, I still feel.

Three months passed and not a word was said about my being sent to school.

Instead, Mrs. Reed had me banished to my room. I took all my meals there alone. Her children were not allowed to speak to me anymore.

Then one day, Bessie burst in. I had just finished eating breakfast—milk and a crusty roll.

"Miss Jane, take off your pinafore and put on a dress," she said. "Someone is here to see you."

I couldn't imagine who that could be.

Other than the people who lived in this house, I did not know a soul in the world.

I went down to the drawing room, not knowing what to expect. A man was standing by the fireplace. He was wearing a long black coat. All I could see at first was his back. He was standing straight and still, and his posture was so stiff, his body so tall and thin, I thought I was looking at a black pillar. Mrs. Reed was sitting on the sofa. When she saw me, she made an impatient motion with her hand, signaling for me to come close.

"This is the little girl I wrote to you about," she said to the stranger.

The stranger turned around to face me. He stared at me hard in silence for a moment, then said to Mrs. Reed, "She's small. What is her age?"

"She's ten years old," Mrs. Reed said.

"What is your name?" the stranger said to me.

"Jane Eyre, sir."

"Well, Jane Eyre," he said. "Are you a good child?"

"She's a bad child, Mr. Brocklehurst," Mrs. Reed said, before I could answer.

"I'm sorry to hear it," Mr. Brocklehurst said. He bent over, so that his face came down to the same level as mine and looked into my eyes. He had a huge nose, gray bushy eyebrows over small round eyes, and a wide mouth with crooked yellow teeth. "You know what happens to bad little girls when they die?" he asked. "They fall into a pit and burn for all eternity, for nothing can extinguish the flames. What must you do to avoid such a fate? Answer me!"

"I must try to stay healthy, so I don't die," I said.

"God decides who stays healthy," he said. "You have to pray day and night. You have to pray to God for forgiveness, and repent your evil ways."

He shook his finger at me, and kept staring solemnly at my face.

"Mr. Brocklehurst," Mrs. Reed said. "As I wrote in my letter to you, and as you yourself now see, she's stubborn and impertinent. But the worst of it is, she's deceitful."

Oh, it was Mrs. Reed who was deceitful! This very moment she was telling a lie. I never lied. But now, Mr. Brocklehurst

was going to believe her and think me a liar. I glanced at his face and saw I was right. He looked at me with disgust.

"Deceit is a terrible fault in a child," he said to Mrs. Reed. "Stay assured, I'll forewarn her teachers, so they keep a close eye on her."

"I want it understood that she will spend her vacations at school," Mrs. Reed said. "I leave her entirely in your care."

"I will send for her as soon as possible," Mr. Brocklehurst said.

"The sooner the better," Mrs. Reed said. "I've had all I can stand of her."

Mr. Brocklehurst bent by the waist and said good-bye. Mrs. Reed and I were left alone.

"Go back to your room," she said, without looking at me.

I started walking toward the door, but suddenly I stopped and turned around. I was beside myself with rage.

"I'm not a liar," I screamed at her. "If I

were, I would say to you I love you. But I don't love you. I hate you more than anybody in the world. It is you and your children who tell lies."

Not a muscle moved on Mrs. Reed's face. She did not even blink.

"Anything more you have to say?" she said.

"Yes. I'm glad you're not related to me by blood. I'd feel ashamed if you were a blood relative of mine. If anyone asks me how I like you and how you treated me, I'll say the very thought of you makes me sick, and that you were cruel and mean to me."

"How dare you speak to me like that, Jane Eyre."

"How dare I? Because it's the truth. Anyone who asks me questions about you, I'll tell them just how you treated me. And I'll tell them how you had me locked up in the red room and did not care that I could die from fright. I won't lie!"

I walked out of the room with my head up, taking slow, sure steps. I had never felt so good in my life. I had stood up for myself and I was proud and glad I'd done it.

Chapter 3
One Good Friend

I don't remember very much about my trip to school. Bessie put me in a coach, gave the driver my destination, and told him to keep an eye on me. I left early in the morning. It was after nightfall when I arrived at the small inn where someone from school was supposed to pick me up. I was cold and hungry, and my body was stiff from the long journey. I kept looking out the window to see who might be walking into the inn, but no one came to fetch me. I had all but given up hope, when I saw a carriage drive up the road. It stopped in front of the inn, the door opened, and an older woman dressed like a servant stepped out.

"Is there a little girl called Jane Eyre here?" she shouted from the street.

"Yes! Yes!" I yelled. "I'm Jane Eyre."

I ran out as fast as I could, afraid that if I didn't get there right away she would think no one had heard her and would leave. Without saying a word, she helped me climb into the carriage.

It was another long journey. For a while, I looked out the window, trying to see the landscape of the area where I would now live, but all I could see was darkness and rain. Soon, lulled by the clopping sound of the horses' hooves, I fell asleep.

Next thing I remember is being lifted out of the carriage in someone's arms and put down in front of a large building. It had many windows, but only a few were lit up. A pebble path led to a broad door. Out of it came a woman whose face I could not see in the dark. She walked up to me, took my hand, and led me into the building.

"The child is too young to have traveled alone," she said to the servant who had picked me up at the inn.

She was a young woman, around twenty-five. She had a sad but kind face and was wearing a plain dress and a frayed shawl over her shoulders. She told me she was a teacher and that her name was Miss Miller, then led me through countless corridors to a long wide room with several large tables in it. It was study hour. Eighty girls, from nine to twenty years old, sat around the tables, each with her head bent over a book. They looked up at me for a second, then back down at their books. They all had pale, drawn faces. Their hair was brushed back, so that there wasn't one loose curl, not one wispy,

stray strand falling on their foreheads. They were wearing dresses made out of coarse brown material, and white starched petticoats. Even the older girls, who were nineteen or twenty years old, were wearing petticoats.

"Monitors, collect the books and put them away!" Miss Miller said.

The tallest girls gathered the books and put them on the shelves.

"Monitors, bring the dinner trays!"

On each tray there was a single mug

of water and a platter of food—I could not see what kind. The girls took sips of water from the same mug and served themselves small portions of food. When they had finished eating, Miss Miller commanded them to read from their prayer books. Then she commanded them to leave the room.

The girls filed out one by one. Miss Miller and I left the room last. We followed the girls up the stairs and into another long wide room, with three long rows of beds. Two girls slept to a bed. Miss Miller told me that I'd have to share her bed. I was so exhausted that I fell asleep right away, and was dead to the world.

I woke up to the sound of a loud bell. Most of the girls had already gotten out of bed and were washing up. There were over a dozen basins in the room; each one had to be shared by six girls who, one after the other, splashed her face with the same water. I waited my turn, shivering in the cold, then dressed up as quickly as I could.

Another bell rang and the girls formed a line, two by two, and marched down the stairs and into a large, dimly lit room. Miss Miller read a prayer, then called out: "Form classes!" The girls sep-arated into groups, and each group sat down at a separate table. There were four tables in all, and the girls had to sit down around them in hard, wooden chairs, with their backs ramrod straight.

"Silence! Silence!" Miss Miller shouted.

Another bell rang, and three more teachers walked into the room. Their faces were plain and severe, with tired, solemn eyes and lips pressed tightly.

The lessons began. The teachers sat down, one at each table, and for one hour we had to read the Bible. Then, another bell rang.

"Form a line and march to the dining room!" Miss Miller said.

Everything was done by command, and before each command the bell rang.

I had been too exhausted and too nervous to eat anything the night before. Now I was ravenous. I did not need a command to sit down and eat. I couldn't wait. But when the food came, it smelled so awful, I could only eat a spoonful.

"It tastes disgusting," one of the oldest girls said. "The porridge is burned again."

None of the girls could eat. The teachers tried to set a good example, but they could not finish their portions.

We marched back to the classroom, with empty stomachs. I was so weak, I thought I'd faint. We all sat around our tables again, and made ready for our lesson. Then the door to the classroom flew open and a tall, beautiful woman walked in. The girls turned their heads and looked at her, and I saw their faces light up with adoration and love. She had a lovely, sweet face, with a high forehead, large brown eyes, and thick hair

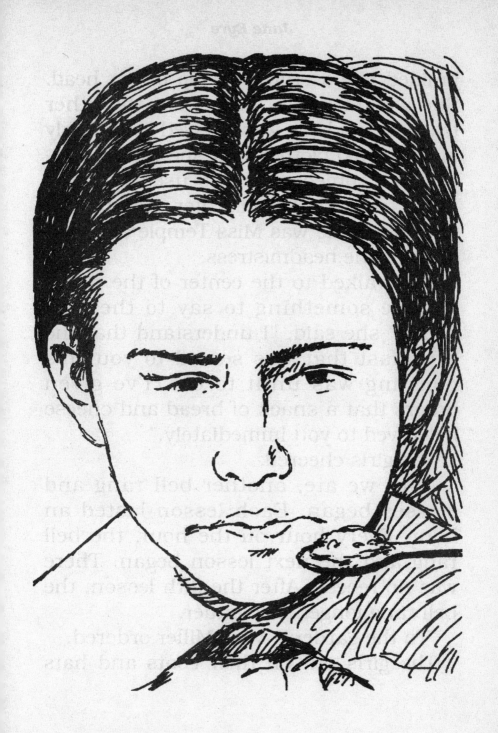

braided like a crown on top of her head. She wasn't much older than the other teachers, and she was dressed in similarly plain, frayed clothes, but she carried herself like someone who is used to being respected and obeyed. Later, I found out that her name was Miss Temple and that she was the headmistress.

She walked to the center of the room. "I have something to say to the students," she said. "I understand that the breakfast that was served to you this morning was unfit to eat. I've given orders that a snack of bread and cheese be served to you immediately."

The girls cheered.

After we ate, another bell rang and classes began. Each lesson lasted an hour. Every hour on the hour, the bell rang and the next lesson began. There was no recess. After the fifth lesson, the bell rang longer and louder.

"To the garden!" Miss Miller ordered.

The girls put on their coats and hats

and streamed out the door. I followed, last to leave the class.

The garden was fenced in by a stone wall, too high to see over. There were several flower beds. No doubt, they looked beautiful in the spring, but now they lay bare. The ground was soaking wet because of last night's rain, and the sky was gray. It was misty and cold. I stood shivering against the wall. No one seemed to

notice me. I was used to feeling lonely, but I had never felt so alone or so miserable. I was still famished, I was freezing from the cold, and I had no one to talk to. The rest of the girls had broken up into groups and were chatting and laughing.

I was beginning to give up hope that I could get close to anyone, when I noticed another girl who sat all alone on the doorsill. She was reading a

book. I walked over to her and asked her what she was reading.

"Oh, it's a novel," she said. She stared thoughtfully at my face. "Are you an orphan?" she asked.

"Yes. Both of my parents died before I can remember. Why do you ask?"

"Most of the girls here are orphans," she said. "All of us are charity cases."

"Do you like the teachers?" I asked.

"Well enough."

"How about Miss Temple?"

"I love Miss Temple. She's wonderful."

"How long have you been here?"

"Two years."

"Are you happy here?"

"You ask too many questions," the girl said. "I want to read."

She looked down at her book, but before she could start reading again the bell rang.

"We have to go back in," she said. "It's time for dinner."

Dinner was some kind of stew made

from stringy, tough meat and potatoes. The portions were large but the food tasted so bad that, famished as I was, I could only eat a little.

Afterwards, we went back to the classroom. The evening lessons went pretty much the way the morning lessons had gone. The only remarkable event was that the girl I had talked to in the garden was punished by the history teacher, Miss Scatcherd. She was not at my table, so I don't know what she had done wrong. The teacher called out her name—which, it turns out, was Helen Burns—and asked her to stand in the middle of the classroom. Everyone in class turned their head and stared, but Helen Burns did not seem to mind. Had it been me, I would have wished that the earth open up and swallow me. Helen Burns did not even blush. There was a far-away look in her eyes, as if she were daydreaming.

I wondered about her. She looked to

be thirteen—quite a bit older and taller than I. She had a serious, gentle face. I had liked her earlier. I had thought she was honest and bright. Could she be a bad girl? If not, why was she punished?

Chapter 4
A Cruel Place

During the next few days, it seemed like a moment did not pass without Miss Scatcherd scolding Helen. "Burns, you're sticking your chin out!" she'd say to her. "Burns, hold your head up!" One time, she asked the class a question. None of the girls knew the answer, except for Helen, but when she raised her hand, Miss Scatcherd said: "You dirty girl! You didn't clean your nails this morning!"

Helen was silent. Why doesn't she explain that the water in the basin was frozen over with ice? I thought. None of us had been able to wash up.

"You're a slob!" Miss Scatcherd said. "When will you learn to be neat!"

That evening, I saw Helen standing by the fireplace in the recreation room. She had the same far-away look in her eyes I had observed the first day. It was as if she lived in a dream, and nothing could touch her.

"You must wish you could leave school," I said.

"Why would I?" she said. "I came here to get an education, and I'll stay till I get one."

"But Miss Scatcherd treats you so badly."

"Badly? Not at all. She's trying to correct my faults."

"But you don't have any faults. You're good."

"I do have faults," Helen said. "I'm

messy. Miss Scatcherd was right to call me a slob. I'm disobedient. I'm absent-minded."

"I don't understand how you can be so calm about it. If it were me, I'd hate her from the bottom of my soul."

"You cannot fight hate with hate. Only love can overcome hatred. It's in the Bible: 'Love your enemies; bless them that curse you; do good to them that hurt you.'"

"According to you, I should love Mrs. Reed then. I should love her son John. Well, I can't! I won't!"

"Who are they?"

I told Helen my story.

"No doubt, Mrs. Reed and her son have been unkind to you," she said. "You have to try to forgive them and forget the hurt. Otherwise, the resentment will poison your heart, and you'll be unhappy your whole life."

After this talk, Helen and I became close friends.

Life at school was hard. All day, every day, we spent our time either in class, or studying. Sundays, we had to get up at dawn, walk to church—two miles in the bitter cold—and attend the morning service. We were served a small snack that was supposed to do for both breakfast and lunch. Then we stayed on for the afternoon service, and afterwards walked back to school. By then, we were weak from hunger and exhaustion. The walk back was uphill and we had to push against the wind that blew down from the snowy mountain ridge. The skin on my face became so raw from the cold that it bled sometimes.

As a special treat, we were given a whole slice of bread, instead of the usual half slice, at tea time. Then, we had to spend the whole evening reading the Bible and listening to a long sermon, which was read to us by one of the teachers. By the time we were ordered to march to the dining hall for supper, we

could barely stand on our feet or keep our eyes open. And that, dear reader, was our day of rest—the one day we did not have to study.

One afternoon, when I had been in school for about three weeks, Miss Temple walked into the classroom, followed by a tall, thin man dressed in black. Before I could see his face, my blood ran cold. I just knew it was Mr.

Brocklehurst. I had never seen another man look so much like a stone pillar.

"Miss Temple," he said. "I've just gone over the accounts. I see that there's been an extra charge for bread and cheese served as a snack."

"Please let me explain," Miss Temple said. "One morning, the porridge was so badly burned, it was inedible. I asked the cook to prepare a snack, or the girls would have had to go without food all day."

"This is a school, Miss Temple. The aim of the school's education is not to pamper the students, but to teach them how to withstand hardship. They should have eaten their burnt porridge. You had no authority to make a substitution of bread and cheese."

He looked at each girl, inspecting their appearance.

"Miss Temple!" he said in an angry voice. "Who is the girl with the red curly hair?"

"It's Julia Severn," Miss Temple replied quietly.

"Why does she have curls? It's not allowed."

"Her hair curls naturally," Miss Temple said.

"Naturally! What sort of an excuse is that! One could say then, in one's defense, that one is naturally a glutton, naturally lazy, naturally a moron. Her hair must be cut off! I'll send in a barber tomorrow."

He continued inspecting the girls. Finally, my turn came.

"Ah, the new pupil!" he said. "What is your name?"

"Jane Eyre, sir."

He asked me to bring a stool, put it in the middle of the room and stand on it. I did as he asked.

"Miss Temple, teachers and children," he said. "Do you all see this girl?"

Of course, they did! They were staring right at me.

"You must be on your guard against her. This girl is a liar. I learned this from the lady who had adopted her—a respectable, kind, generous lady. She was forced to send her away to this school because she did not want her around her own children."

My skin was burning with shame.

"You are to stand on the stool for half an hour," he said to me. "No one is allowed to talk to you for the rest of the day."

He left the room.

The girls went back to their lessons. When the half hour was up, Miss Miller asked me to take my place back at the table where my class sat. I did, but no one raised their eyes to look at me. Then, when the bell rang for recess, they all avoided me.

I walked to the far side of the garden, sat on the ground, hugging my knees with my arms, and wept.

"Shhh—" I heard a soft voice say.

It was Helen.

"Oh, Helen! Everyone believes that I'm a liar."

"Who is everyone?" Helen said. "There are eighty girls in this school. The school is not the whole world. The world contains millions and millions of people."

"What do I care about the millions and millions? All I know is eighty people. Of these eighty people, everyone despises me."

"You're wrong, Jane. Not one of the girls despises or even dislikes you. They pity you, that's all. They know Mr. Brocklehurst is an unfair man. But, let's say they did hate and despise you. What does it matter, if your conscience is clear? A clear conscience is all the friend one needs."

"I can't bear it to have people hate me," I said. "I can't bear it to feel alone. I would rather have every single bone of my body broken than be alone. I want people to love me, Helen. I want people to think well of me."

"Hush, hush—God loves you, Jane. God loves us all."

Helen put her arms around me, and I felt better. She loved me. It did not matter, suddenly, that no one else loved me.

Chapter 5
Death Visits

Spring came. The garden looked beautiful. Flowers were beginning to peep out among the leaves. Everything was green. On sunny days, the air was bright with light and soft with warmth. Life did not seem so hard any more. Partly, it was the joy of spring. Partly, it was because there were no classes. Many of the students had become sick and the teachers had to take on the duty of nurses. Those of the students who remained healthy spent their free time unsupervised.

I did not give much thought to the sick girls, at first. They were taken to the infirmary and stayed there for days. They had the flu or spring colds, I thought. But it was typhus fever, dear reader. Many of the girls died. The school began to smell like a hospital. The dark corridors, that had always been gloomy, now seemed like tunnels leading to death. When I walked through them, I shivered with fear.

I spent most of my time in the garden. Because so many of the girls had died or were too sick to eat, there was an abundance of food. Each meal was like a feast. I ate with great appetite and relish. I became stronger—robust, despite my slight frame. With my body, my spirits, too, improved. I felt happier. I became less shy. I made new friends. There was one girl in particular I liked a lot, and she and I became inseparable

after a while. Her name was Ann Wilson. She was a great gossip and very clever. I knew she was shallow, but she was so much fun to be around I did not care.

And what about Helen?

Helen was one of the girls who had become ill. She did not have typhus, however. She suffered from consumption. All I knew about consumption, dear reader, was that one coughed a lot. I thought it was no more serious than a cold, so I did not worry.

Late one evening, I was playing with Ann in the garden, when we saw Dr. Bates, the village doctor, come through the gate. We knew someone must be close to death. Dr. Bates made his rounds early each morning. If he made an appearance at any other time, it meant someone was very ill.

"I wonder who he's come for," I said.

I felt scared. When the doctor came back out, Miss Miller followed behind him. She walked him to the gate. I ran

up to her. Something about the worried way with which she looked at me made me ask: "Is it Helen Burns?"

"Yes, Jane. She's terribly ill. Dr. Bates said she won't be with us long."

At first, I thought she meant that Helen was going to be sent back home. Then, with horror, I realized she meant Helen was about to die.

"I want to see her!" I cried. "I want to go to the infirmary."

"She's not in the infirmary," Miss

Miller said. "She's in Miss Temple's room. You can't see her. It's not allowed."

I had to see her! I was determined. That night, I waited till everyone was asleep, and stole out of the dormitory. The lights were out and I had to walk down the corridor in the scary dark. Miss Temple's room was at the other end of the building. My heart beat fast, and I was shivering from the cold because I only had on my nightgown.

The air smelled of camphor and disinfectant. It was a sickening smell but I was grateful for it. It was my guide: the stronger the smell became, the closer I was coming to the room.

When I finally got to it, I saw that the door was ajar. I was scared—scared that Miss Temple might be there and send me away; scared that Helen might already be dead. I had wanted to say good-bye. I had wanted to hug her before she died.

I must see her, I thought.

There was a small candle burning on the bureau. I could see Miss Temple's bed and next to it a narrow cot, on which Helen was lying motionless.

"Helen," I whispered. "Helen, are you awake?"

She stirred weakly, and slowly opened her eyes.

"Jane, is it you?" she said.

She's not going to die, I thought. She wouldn't be able to stir at all if she were dying. She wouldn't be able to speak. Her face would not look so calm.

I got into bed with her, covered myself up with the blanket and kissed her. Her cheek was icy cold. She smiled at me, the way she always did when she saw me.

"What are you doing here, Jane? It's the middle of the night."

"I came to see you," I said.

"Ah—you came to say good-bye. You're just in time."

"Are you going somewhere? Are you going home?"

"Yes," she said. "My true home—my last home."

"Don't say that! Don't say that!" I cried.

"Don't be upset, Jane. I'm very happy. When you hear I'm dead, I don't want you to be sad. There's nothing to be sad about. We'll all die one day. We suffer while we live, but when we die there's no more suffering. I've had a short life, so I haven't suffered much. That's a good thing. I'm going to be with God now. God loves me. God loves us all. Heaven, God's home, is a happy place."

"Will I see you again, when I die? Will we be friends again—in heaven?"

"Yes, Jane. We will."

I put my arms around her and held her tight.

"How nice and warm you feel," she said. "I'm tired and I want to sleep.

Promise me you'll stay the night. I don't want you to leave. It's so good to have you near me."

"I promise."

"Are you comfortable, Jane? Is there enough room? Are you warm enough?"

"I'm comfortable."

"Well, then. Good night."

We kissed. In a short while, we were both asleep.

At dawn, when Miss Temple returned to her room from the infirmary, where she had spent the night, she found me lying on the cot. My face was against Helen Burns' shoulder, my arms around her neck. I was asleep. Helen was dead.

Chapter 6
Leaving for Work

The number of students who died that year brought to light the inhumane and unsanitary conditions under which the school was run. Mr. Brocklehurst was replaced by a new inspector, who was a fair and kind man. The patrons donated greater sums of money, so that the girls could be fed well. The school became an excellent institution.

Still, it was like living in a prison. I was proud to be first in my class, glad that the teachers treated me with respect and love, happy that I had made good friends, grateful that I did not have to worry about having a roof over my head. But what good is all that without freedom?

I wanted to live in the world. I wanted to learn about the world. I was intelligent, capable, healthy. I did not want to be a charity case. Who said that because I was a woman I could not be independent and earn my living?

After I finished school, I stayed on for two more years as a teacher, then I made up my mind to leave. I was twenty years old. It was time, I thought, to be on my own. So, I put an advertisement in the paper, saying I was seeking a position as a governess. I did not have to wait long. In a little over a week, a position was offered to me. I was to take care of a ten-year-old girl.

Reader, you cannot imagine how I felt. For ten years, I had not gone beyond the

walls of the school. Mrs. Reed, my step-mother had stated that she did not want me "to darken her doorstep" again, so that during summers and holidays, there had been nowhere for me to go. The last time I had been on a coach was when I first came to the school. I had been frightened then, and I was as frightened now. I did not know what might be in store for me. All the information that I had consisted of two names: "Mrs. Fairfax," the name of the lady who had responded to my ad, and "Thornfield," the name of the place where she lived.

I arrived in early evening, after a sixteen-hour journey. All I could make out in the dark was the outline of a large, gloomy building. Candlelight gleamed from a bay window on the ground floor; everything else was dark. A servant opened the door when I knocked, and, without saying a word, she led me to a small room. An elderly lady sat by the fireplace. I assumed she was the lady of the house, and I was surprised to see that she had no airs but greeted me with a warm and kindly smile.

"How do you do, my dear?" she said. "You must be awfully tired."

"Are you Mrs. Fairfax?" I asked.

"Yes, I am. Come sit down close to me, by the fire. You must be freezing. Do you have any luggage?"

"Yes."

"I'll see that it's taken up to your room," she said, leaving me alone for a moment.

She was treating me like a guest. I had expected a cold, stiff reception. I had heard that governesses were treated just a little better than servants. When she returned I asked her when I would be meeting Miss Fairfax.

She looked confused. "Miss Fairfax?" she said.

"My pupil."

"Ah! You mean Miss Varens."

Now it was I who was confused. "She's not your daughter?"

"Good heavens, no!"

No further explanation was given on the matter. A servant brought us tea and sandwiches, and while we ate, Mrs. Fairfax told me how much I'd like Thornfield.

"It's a little dreary in the winter, but what place isn't? In any case, Adele—

that is Miss Varens's name—makes the place quite lively. And the grounds are lovely, you'll see. Of course, they're not kept as well as they would be, if Mr. Rochester resided here all the time."

"Who is Mr. Rochester?" I asked.

"The owner of Thornfield," she said.

"I thought Thornfield belonged to you."

"What an idea!" Mrs. Fairfax said. "I am the housekeeper."

"Who are Adele's parents?" I asked.

"Adele is Mr. Rochester's ward. Her mother is French and lives in France."

Without further explanation, Mrs. Fairfax showed me to my room.

The next morning, when I met Adele, I saw that she was a pretty, charming child. She did not like to work hard, but she was docile and sweet-tempered. I liked her, and I liked Mrs. Fairfax. The room where I slept was cozy and cheerful. The library, which Mr. Rochester had ordered to be used as a schoolroom, was filled with interesting books. There was plenty to read. The countryside was beautiful, and I enjoyed taking long walks each day.

And yet, there was something creepy about living in an immense, empty house. There were countless rooms that were kept closed. The large hallways echoed with my footsteps when I walked about. The whole upper floor was unoccupied, but late at night strange, eerie sounds came from it. I knew it was the

wind—strong drafts sweeping through the empty rooms—but could have sworn I heard footsteps and, sometimes, shrieks.

I had been taught drawing at school. It was something I had excelled at, and now I took it up again. I got in the habit of going up to the roof to draw the view of the countryside from up high. On one such day, as I walked up the narrow staircase that went past the attic, I heard a loud screeching laugh. I stopped

in front of the attic door and listened carefully. The person who had laughed before laughed again, in a lower tone. Then, there was total silence.

There had been no joy in the laughter. It was shrill, vicious, mocking. It made my blood run cold. Instead of going on up to the roof, I ran back downstairs.

"Mrs. Fairfax," I said out of breath. "There's someone in the attic! I heard someone laughing."

"Oh," said Mrs. Fairfax calmly. "That must have been Grace Poole. She's one of the servants. She goes up there to sew."

Who is Grace Poole? I thought. How come I've never seen her? Why would she go up to the attic to sew?

Chapter 7
Mr. Rochester

People say that all that a woman wants is a quiet, safe life. I don't believe it. I had just such a life, and I wasn't satisfied. Women feel just like men feel. They want excitement and adventure in their lives. They need to challenge and enlarge their minds. How can anyone suppose that a woman is happy staying all day inside the house?

I had thought my life would change when I left school. It was the reason I had wanted to leave. Now, here I was and I still felt like I was living in a prison—a beautiful prison, a mansion of a prison. What difference did it make? Day in and day out, it was the same routine: I taught Adele her lessons, I went up to the roof to draw, I had lunch and dinner with Mrs. Fairfax—a nice woman but not a great conversationalist—I took long walks in the garden, I read, and I went to bed.

October, November, December passed. January came. One morning, Adele woke up with a cold. I decided that she should stay in bed, so there were no lessons that day. I sat in the library and read. In the afternoon, Mrs. Fairfax said she had a letter she needed to post, so I volunteered to take it to the post office in the village. It was a chance to get out of the house, and I jumped at it.

It was a brisk, two-mile walk. The day was particularly cold but the sky was clear and the scenery shone in the

bright sunlight. Cows were grazing in the fields, and little birds perched on the bare tree branches, looking like brown leaves that had forgotten to fall. I came to a stretch of the road that was covered with ice. I stopped, afraid to go forward. Just as I was standing there, thinking that maybe I should cross over the field instead, I heard a horse coming. The area was completely deserted, and the clopping sound of the hooves came from around the bend of the road. I had heard that there was a spirit called "Gytrash" that haunted the road. It took on the form of a horse and galloped around solitary travelers, scaring them to death. I imagined a wild horse with red eyes, a mane like a lion's, and cloven hooves like the devil's. But it was an ordinary horse that appeared. A man was riding on it. I was relieved, though my heart still beat fast.

As the horse reached the ice, it took a fall, throwing the rider. The man tried to get back up on his feet, but kept slipping on the ice.

"Are you hurt, sir?" I asked, going near him to help.

He groaned with pain, and did not reply.

"Can I do anything, sir?" I asked.

"Don't just stand there. Give me a hand," he said rudely.

His rudeness did not offend me. It was clear he was in pain. I gave him my

hand, and he pulled himself up. He felt his legs and arms.

"No bones broken," he said. "Just a sprain."

He was of medium height but had broad shoulders and a stocky body. He looked to be about thirty-five. No one would call him handsome, but he had beautiful dark eyes and a strong, manly face. He acted rough, but I could tell he was not unkind.

"What are you doing out here?" he said. "You shouldn't be out alone in such a deserted place."

"I live quite near," I said. "At Thornfield Hall, if you know it."

He gave no sign that he knew it.

"You're not a servant there," he said.

"The governess."

"I see."

He asked me to take his horse by the bridle and bring it over. Then, leaning on my shoulder, he mounted the saddle.

"Necessity compels me to accept your

offer of help," he said. "Hand me my whip. It lies under the hedge. That will be all. Thank you."

He galloped towards Thornfield, without giving me one more glance.

I went on to the village, mailed Mrs. Fairfax's letter and hurried back. The sun was setting when I reached the gate. It wasn't that dark yet, but the windows of the house were ablaze with candlelight. When I entered, the front hall was bright with light coming through the doors of the large dining room.

I stood still with amazement.

Mrs. Fairfax came out of the dining room, saw the expression on my face, and smiled.

"Mr. Rochester has just come home," she said. "He's now with the doctor. Apparently, he had a fall and sprained his ankle."

I went up to my room to take off my coat, then down to the library.

"Oh no, miss," the maid told me.

"When the master is home, that's where the master sits."

Mrs. Fairfax explained that from now on I should be using the parlor on the second floor.

I had supper that night alone. The next morning, I was at my wit's end, trying to keep Adele in hand.

"Mr. Rochester is home! Mr. Rochester is home!" she kept saying. "He's brought me a trunk full of presents. I saw it!"

She prattled on and on. The trunk contained a doll . . .the trunk contained a doll house . . .the trunk contained new dresses. . . .

I did not see Mrs. Fairfax all day. She

was too busy. Now that Mr. Rochester was here, she had many more things to see to. The rooms that had been unused all these months had to be aired out and dusted. More groceries had to be ordered, larger meals prepared. Neighbors came to pay their respects, or to discuss business. What with the endless parade of visitors, what with the servants bustling about to keep everything in order, there was constant commotion.

Finally, that evening, I was called downstairs.

"Oh no, Miss Eyre," Mrs. Fairfax said. "You have to change your dress. Mr. Rochester would like you and Adele to take tea with him."

I went back to my room and put on the one nice dress I had. It was a simple black silk dress. The only jewelry I possessed was a small pin made of pearls that Miss Temple had given me as a good-bye gift. I wore it, hoping it would

make the dress look nicer. Before going
out the door, I glanced at myself swiftly
in the mirror. What was the use of staring longer at my face? I was plain. I
knew I was plain.

I took a few steps into the large drawing room, and stood still. Mr. Rochester
was lying on a sofa, resting his sprained
ankle on a cushion. Adele was sitting on
the floor by his feet. Mrs. Fairfax sat in a
straight-back chair near the fireplace.

I did not know how to proceed. I knew Mr. Rochester was aware that I had entered the room and was standing a few feet away from him, but he did not turn his head toward me, as though he was not in the mood to notice anyone.

"Miss Eyre is here, sir," Mrs. Fairfax said.

He bowed. "Let Miss Eyre be seated," he said.

With the cold formal way in which he said it and with the forced, stiff way in which he bowed, it was as if he were really saying: "I don't give a hoot that she's here or not here."

Reader, his rudeness set me at ease. Had he been polite, had he acted like a true gentleman, I would have felt shy. I did not have a refined, high-society manner to respond to a gentleman in kind. Rudeness, I could deal with. Besides, I liked him for being rude. Rudeness is not hypocritical the way politeness often is.

For a while, no one spoke or moved. A servant brought in the tea, and Mrs. Fairfax poured.

"Will you hand Mr. Rochester his tea?" she said to me. "I'd ask Adele but I'm afraid she'd spill it."

I did as I was told. Mr. Rochester took the cup from my hand, without looking at me.

"What brought you here, Miss Eyre?" he said.

"I needed a job."

"Of course, you needed a job. You wouldn't be working, unless you needed a job. What brought you to Thornfield Hall?"

"I advertised in the paper, and Mrs. Fairfax answered my ad."

"And how lucky that was!" said Mrs. Fairfax. "It's been just wonderful to have Miss Eyre here. She's been an excellent companion for me, and a great teacher for Adele."

"Mrs. Fairfax," said Mr. Rochester, "I did not ask you for a character reference. I can judge Miss Eyre's character for myself. Already I know that she scared my horse and made me fall. I have to thank her for this sprain."

It was hard to tell whether he was joking or not.

"So," he said. "What were you doing out on the road? Who were you waiting for?"

"I was on my way to the village to post a letter for Mrs. Fairfax," I said.

He turned his face to me and stared. Could it be my imagination, reader? I thought I saw a sudden softness in his eyes. In a moment, it was gone. He turned his face away.

"Do you play the piano?" he said, without looking at me.

"A little."

"Everyone plays a little," he said. "Go into the library and play something for me."

I obeyed.

"Enough!" he called out after a few

minutes. "You play like any other young woman. Perhaps, better than some, but not well."

I closed the piano and went back.

"I understand you can draw," he said. "Let me see some of your drawings."

I went up to my room and brought back some of my drawings.

"You have some talent," he said. He looked through the drawings I had given him, and handed them back to me. "Talent, but not much skill. Now, you may leave. And take the child with you."

Adele went to kiss him good night. He turned to her a stony cheek, then pushed her off him the way one does a dog that's making a nuisance of itself.

"I wish you both a good night," he said.

He might as well have said, "dismissed." I curtsied, received a frigid bow in return, took Adele by the hand, and left the room.

After I put Adele to bed, I went to Mrs. Fairfax's room and waited for her. I wanted to get some information about Mr. Rochester. He had piqued my interest, to say the least.

This is what I learned: He had been the master of Thornfield Hall for the last nine years, since the death of his older brother. Till his brother's death, he had chosen to live abroad where, it was said, he had led a dissolute life. While living in Paris, he befriended an opera singer who had a young child, Adele. When Mr. Rochester realized that the child was

neglected and mistreated, he decided to take her away and give her a good home at Thornfield Hall.

Only a good man would take it upon himself to take care of a neglected child, I thought. And yet, he did not show any true affection toward the poor girl. I could not make him out.

Chapter 8
A Fire!

For the next few days, he was busy
taking care of his affairs, visiting his
neighbors or receiving visits. The only
times I saw him, it was by chance,
when our paths crossed—in the hall-
way, the stairs, or out on the grounds.
He would glance at me, bow, and move
on, barely acknowledging my presence.
His face seemed clouded over, his eyes
bitter and angry.

One evening, after more than two

weeks had passed, I was asked to take tea with him again.

"I want to spend some time with Adele this evening," he said. "I am a bachelor and I'm not used to children. I haven't the vaguest idea what one is to do with them. I find children irritating and their conversation boring. Your presence will help."

His ankle had mended and he was sitting in a large armchair. Adele was sitting on a small stool by his feet, looking up at his face adoringly. Mrs. Fairfax was pouring tea. I sat down next to her on the sofa.

"You're staring at me, Miss Eyre," he said. "Do you think I'm handsome?"

"No, sir."

"By God, Miss Eyre! Are you always so blunt? What fault do you find with my features, pray?"

"No fault, sir. It's your general demeanor."

"I see. Well, you're no more pretty

than I am handsome," he said. "What do you have to say for yourself?"

I was silent.

"Have you been struck dumb suddenly, Miss Eyre?"

"Sir, ask me questions and I will do my best to answer them."

"Do you ever laugh?"

"When I have occasion to," I said.

"Ha! I bet that when you laugh, you laugh from your heart. You're no more severe by nature than I am vicious."

"I don't think you're vicious, sir."

"Ah, Miss Eyre! I was born a good man. I used to be good. I used to be loving and trusting. But I was wronged by my brother. I was deceived—played for a fool. Now, I'm bitter and hard. When I saw goodness did not pay, I turned to vice. I've led an immoral life."

"Surely not, sir," I said. "You look to me to be honorable and honest. Admitting you are a bad man, shows you have a conscience."

"That I do, and it tells me I'm bad."

The sadness and regret with which he spoke those words moved me deeply.

"If you know you were good once, you can be good again," I said. "Listen to your conscience. Do what it tells you to do."

"My conscience cannot erase the past," he said.

"Repentance can," I said.

He did not reply. Then, abruptly, he said: "It's time for Adele to go to bed. Good night, Miss Eyre."

After that night, whenever he ran into me, he stared straight at my face. His eyes had a sad, questioning look that I did not fully understand. It was as though he expected to see something in my eyes—some expression or sign. I smiled at him but he didn't smile back. He kept staring at me in a way that made me lower my eyes.

I was falling in love with him, reader. Don't think that I had become blind to

his faults. He was proud, cynical,
gloomy, dictatorial, harsh. But I knew
there was great kindness and nobility in
him. He was a bitter, disappointed man.
Not a bad man. He suffered, and took
his unhappiness out on others.

Days went by when I did not see him
at all. But he was always on my mind.
At night, it was hard for me to sleep
because I kept thinking of him. What if
he goes away? I thought. He did not

seem to like Thornfield Hall. Mrs. Fairfax had told me that he never stayed for long.

One night, I felt particularly unhappy. I was convinced he'd leave soon. I won't be able to bear it, I thought. It took me a long time to fall asleep and when I did, it was a very light sleep, such as when one doesn't surely now if one is dreaming or awake. It seemed to me someone was moving about in my room, and I heard a

murmur. I sat up in my bed and listened carefully. The clock in the large hall struck two times. It was exactly two in the morning. There was complete silence, then I heard the door to my room open and close, then the sound of footsteps. My blood ran cold with fear.

"Who's there?" I asked.

No one answered. The sound of footsteps became fainter and fainter. Whoever had been in my room had left.

I fell asleep again. It could only have been for a minute or two. I was woken up again by the sound of laughter. It was the most horrifying laughter I had ever heard—shrill and mean. It reminded me of the laughter I had heard up in the attic. Could it be Grace Poole? If so, what was she doing, roaming the house in the middle of the night?

I ran out of my room to wake up Mrs. Fairfax. I saw that someone had left a candlestick, with a candle burning in it, on the floor just outside my door. I

stared at it, bewildered. I couldn't see the flame clearly. There was smoke obscuring it. How could a candle make so much smoke? I raised my eyes and realized that the smoke was all around. Something was burning!

Panicked, I hurried down the hall with the candle and saw that the smoke was coming from Mr. Rochester's room. I rushed in. Tongues of flame darted around the bed and up the curtains.

"Wake up! Wake up!" I cried. He did not move.

There was not a moment to lose. His sheets were beginning to catch fire. I pulled down the curtains and smothered the flames on the floor. Fortunately, his wash basin and pitcher were filled with water. I emptied them both over him.

"Is there a flood?" he murmured groggily. "Jane! Is that Jane?" he said, coming fully awake. "What are you doing here?"

"There's been a fire, sir. Someone set your bed on fire."

He did not seem shocked that there had been an attempt on his life.

"Let me get some dry clothes on," he said calmly. "While I do so, go fetch a candle. I can barely see my hand in front of my face."

When I came back with the candle, he asked me to sit down next to him on the bed and explain everything that had happened. I told him.

"Should I go wake Mrs. Fairfax?"

"Mrs. Fairfax! Why on earth should you wake up Mrs. Fairfax? Wait for me here. I'll go find out what happened."

He came back a few minutes later, looking deathly pale.

"Everything is all right now," he said.

"Was it Grace Poole?"

He hesitated before answering, then he said: "Yes. It was Grace Poole. She's a little peculiar, as you must have guessed. I've taken care of the situation. There's nothing for you to worry about. I want you to promise me you will not talk to anyone about this incident. Let it stay between us. I'll figure out a way to explain the burnt sheets to Mrs. Fairfax."

"I won't say a word."

"Very well, then. I suppose you want to go back to bed. You must need your sleep. Good night."

"Good night, sir."

He seemed surprised that I was about to leave.

"You're leaving!" he said. "Just like that!"

"Like what, sir? You said I should leave. You bid me good night."

"Yes, yes. But are you going to walk away from me, as if I were a stranger? You've just saved my life."

"I'm glad I happened to be awake, sir." I turned to leave.

"You really want to go so soon, Jane?" he asked. "Won't you talk to me for awhile?"

"I am cold, sir."

"You don't look cold. Why, you're flushed."

He took hold of my hand.

I pulled away. "I think I can hear Mrs.

Fairfax move about in her room, sir," I said. "I think she's awake."

"Well, leave then," he said, letting go of my hand.

Reader, I left. I went back to my room and lay on my bed. He loves me! I thought. He loves me! It was as if I were floating on a sea of joy. But it wasn't a calm sea. In the wake of each wave of joy, there was an undertow of despair. How could I hope he would want to marry me? I was plain and penniless. He was the master of Thornfield Hall.

Chapter 9
Guests in the House

I did not sleep the whole night. In the morning, when I went down to the kitchen, I saw a servant I had never seen before. She was forty or so, with gray hair and a ruddy complexion. She was sitting by the fire, her head bent low, holding a piece of fabric on her lap, which she was busy sewing. I was wondering if she might be Grace Poole, when one of the other servants, as if reading my mind, said: "I don't believe you have met Grace Poole, miss."

Grace Poole raised her face from her sewing. She looked somewhat severe but utterly calm. There was nothing on her face to suggest that this was a mad-woman who had attempted murder a few hours earlier.

Just then, Mrs. Fairfax entered the room. "Did you hear, Miss Eyre?" she asked. "Mr. Rochester almost burned himself to death last night. He forgot to blow out his candle before going to sleep, and his bed caught fire."

"I heard some strange noise," I said, staring at Grace Poole. But nothing in her face had changed expression. Quietly, she had gone back to her sewing.

"Is Grace Poole peculiar?" I asked Mrs. Fairfax later, when we were alone.

"Peculiar? No. She just keeps to herself."

I did not understand why Mr. Rochester would keep her on staff after this last murderous act. It didn't make sense

I didn't see him all day. Surely, he'll ask me to have tea with him this evening, I thought. The evening came and went. I neither heard from him nor saw him.

The next morning while I was having breakfast with Mrs. Fairfax, she said to me: "You haven't touched your food, Miss Eyre. Are you feeling poorly?"

"I never felt better."

"You look so pale. Did you sleep well last night?"

"I never slept better."

"Oh well," Mrs. Fairfax said. "Maybe it's the change in weather. It's such a beautiful spring day—perfect for Mr. Rochester's journey."

"Journey!" I said, trying to conceal my despair. "Why, is he going some place?"

"He's already gone. He'll be away for two or three weeks. He's visiting Lord Ingram. I think he must have decided to

get himself a wife. Lord Ingram has three daughters, all of them beautiful. But, I think, Mr. Rochester has his heart set on the youngest, Blanche. She's a perfect match for him."

"Why is that?"

"She looks grand like a queen—she's as imposing and proud as Mr. Rochester is. She's tall, has lovely sloping shoulders, large dark eyes that shine like jewels, and the longest, glossiest black curly hair you can imagine."

I thought I was going to be sick with

despair. I excused myself and went to my room. You fool! I thought. You silly woman! How could you have thought Mr. Rochester had taken an interest in you? What do you have that can please a man, any man, let alone a gentleman of great wealth and fortune? Look at your limp mousy hair, look at your pale complexion, look at your thin, small body. I covered my face and cried in shame.

In the three weeks that he was away,

I managed to calm myself. Whenever I yearned for him, whenever I felt love rushing to my heart, I stopped it. Just be grateful you have a good job, I said to myself. He's your employer and nothing more.

All this time, there had been no news of Mr. Rochester. At last, word came that Thornfield Hall should be made ready to receive a large party of guests: Lord Ingram and his family, Mr. Eshton, Sir George Lynn, Colonel Dent and their families, and several other people whose names I did not catch. Each guest would be bringing a retinue of servants. Upwards of fifty people altogether were expected.

For days, Thornfield Hall was in an uproar. Rooms had to be aired out, linen had to be washed and ironed, furniture had to be polished, floors had to be scrubbed and waxed.

At last, the day came when the guests arrived. I watched from my win-

dow to see if I could spot Miss Ingram, but all I could see of the ladies from above was large hats with plumes and fluttering veils.

Poor little Adele expected that she would be presented to the guests right away. She kept trying on different dresses, begging me to fix her hair in new ways. For hours, she looked at her little face in the mirror, pouting, smiling—trying on expressions. But no invitation came that

day, nor the next, or next. The guests were to remain for three weeks. The whole first week had passed and Adele had yet to be asked to go downstairs and mingle with the guests.

All this time, I did not come face to face with Mr. Rochester even once. I saw him several times from a distance, however, riding in the company of the same woman. She had long, black curly hair. It must be Miss Ingram, I thought. I could see they were chatting and laughing, as they rode. I had never heard Mr. Rochester laugh, and it made my heart sink to see him laugh now.

At last, the day came when Adele was asked to join the party. I dressed her up and sent her down. A few minutes later, Mrs. Fairfax came to my room and said that Mr. Rochester demanded that I go down as well.

"Wear something nice, my dear. And hurry!" she said.

Something nice! I only had that one good dress, and it was black and buttoned all the way to the neck. I brushed my hair to give it some shine, then pulled it back, twisting it in a tight bun. I looked so drab, I hoped that no one would notice me.

The room was full of people—standing, milling about, seated in chairs. With their finery and jewels, they looked like a flock of brightly plumed birds—some perched on chairs, some standing with their chests puffed out. Their laughter sounded like cackling, their prattle like chirping. They were bird-brained, too— from what I could gather from their talk.

I looked around the room, trying to find Mr. Rochester. I remembered how he had looked the last time we had been together, after the fire in his room—how his face had glowed with love—and my heart started beating loud and fast.

At last, I spotted him among his

guests. He was superior to them by far. He had substance and depth. He had true dignity. His features were harsh—jutting eyebrows and a square chin, a firm, willful mouth, sunken eyes—but how they softened when he smiled! How bright and gentle and sweet his eyes became! When the other men smiled, their smile was like a graceful grimace. It revealed nothing of their soul, as if they had none.

Oh, God! I thought. I still love him!

He was aware of my presence but was acting as if he did not want to see me. He was paying full attention to Miss Ingram, as if there was no one else in the room.

Miss Ingram was pointing to Adele.

"So, this is your ward?" she said. "I suppose you have a governess for her?"

"Yes, I do," Mr. Rochester said. "She must be somewhere in the room."

"I couldn't stand any of my governesses," Miss Ingram said. "They were nasty, or they were plain, stupid, and ridiculous." She turned her face to Adele, gave her a swift, indifferent glance and said, "What an adorable child!"

Mr. Rochester took her by the elbow and led her toward the library.

He's in love with her, I thought. He wants to be alone with her.

Much as it hurt me to realize this, I was relieved. Now I could go back to my room. I had obeyed his command to come down, and he had seen that I had. There was no more reason for me to stay.

Reader, I wanted to cry. Blanche Ingram was very beautiful, indeed. But she was vain and mean. She did not love Mr. Rochester. I could see she was a woman who did not love anyone but herself. She'll make him unhappy, I thought. He's not a man who can love beauty alone. He needs to love a woman who has heart, who has soul. He needs a woman who is as passionate and intel-

ligent as he is, a woman who can appreciate him and understand him. I slipped out the door. No one had noticed me go in; no one noticed me leave. I was about to breathe a sigh of relief when, as I was turning the corner of the corridor, I came face to face with Mr. Rochester.

"Miss Eyre! How do you do?" he said.

"I am very well, sir."

"Why did you not come and speak to me in the drawing room?"

I thought that was the question I should be asking him. Nevertheless, I answered: "I did not wish to disturb you, sir. You were talking with someone."

"What have you been doing to keep yourself busy?"

"Teaching Adele, as usual."

"You look paler than usual," he said. "What's the matter?"

"Nothing at all, sir."

"You're sure you didn't catch cold the night you half-drowned me?"

"I'm sure," I said. "I'm in perfect health."

"If you're feeling so well, why did you leave the gathering?"

"I'm tired, sir."

"You don't look tired," he said. "You look depressed. Tell me, what's bothering you?"

"Nothing at all, sir. I'm happy."

"Why, just now, your eyes brimmed over with tears," he said. "Talk to me!" His eyes had suddenly softened, his face had turned pale. "Talk to me!" he said again.

I looked away.

"Miss Eyre," he said softly. "I see that you want to be alone. I excuse you this time. But understand that as long as my visitors stay here, I expect to see you in the drawing room every evening. Now, good night, my—" He stopped mid-sentence, bit his lip, turned away from me abruptly and went back to the drawing room.

Chapter 10
The Proposal

How different Thornfield Hall had become! There wasn't one room that stood empty. You couldn't walk down a single corridor without coming across some lady's maid or some gentleman's valet. Each evening the drawing room, the dining room, the library, and the parlor were filled with guests in splendid clothes. Hundreds of jewels reflected the candlelight like stars. Amidst all this, I sat silent and unnoticed in some corner, observing Mr. Rochester court Miss Ingram. Reader, it was like torture.

At last, the guests left. I did not see Mr. Rochester for a few days and it began to seem as though he deliberately avoided me. Among the servants, who were always first to know the gossip, nothing was said about his future marriage. I tried to find out from Mrs. Fairfax whether he had proposed, but she was mute on the subject.

One evening I took a walk in the garden. By a large chestnut tree, there was a bench on which I sat to watch the sun set. I happened to like that particular spot because it was in an area where the ground sloped, and no one could see me. The air smelled of jasmine. I breathed in deeply, and smelled another smell—familiar and strange at once. Suddenly, my heart started beating fast. It was the smoke from Mr. Rochester's

cigar! How could it be? I hadn't heard footsteps. I wanted to get up and run, but since I couldn't see up the slope, I might run straight into him. I determined that the best thing to do was walk up slowly. There was thick shrubbery and trees all around, and, if I made no noise, I could walk by him unnoticed.

But he saw me. It seemed as if he had been waiting for me.

"It's such a lovely night," he said. "One doesn't want to stay inside."

I lowered my head, trying to hide the agitation on my face.

"Jane," he said. "There's something I want to talk to you about. I've decided to send Adele away to school."

"I understand, sir. Now that you'll be married you'll want to have children of your own."

"Quite so."

"I understand you won't be needing my services anymore. I'll advertise for a new position right away."

"Does that upset you, Jane?"

"Yes, sir. I'll be sorry to go."

"Sorry because you'll miss Thornfield?"

"Sorry because I'll miss you, sir."

I said it without thinking, because it came from the heart. Tears flooded my eyes, but I was unable to quiet my sobbing.

"Why would you want to leave me then?" he asked.

"Want to? You said I must."

"I said no such thing," he said. "I want you to stay at Thornfield. I want you to be with me—forever."

"What about your wife, sir? What about your marriage?"

"What wife?" he said. "What marriage?"

"Miss Ingram, sir."

"Miss Ingram!" he said. "What do I have to do with Miss Ingram! It's you I want to marry, Jane. You! Will you be mine? Say yes, quickly!"

"Do you truly love me, sir?"

"I do. I swear it."

"Yes, I will marry you, sir."

"Edward," he said. "Call me Edward."

He kissed me over and over. He held me in his arms tightly, saying softly, "My Jane, my darling Jane—"

I pushed him away.

"If you love me—if you knew you loved me, why did you court Miss Ingram?

Why did you let everyone believe you two intended to marry?"

"I wanted to make you jealous," he said. "I wanted to make sure you loved me."

"Oh, Edward! That was so unfair to Miss Ingram."

"Unfair!" he said. "She didn't care a whit about me—only pretended. All Miss Ingram ever liked about me was my wealth."

I laid my head on his shoulder and smiled.

"Let's get back," he said. "Let's go home, my love."

Home, I thought. Home! Thornfield Hall was going to be my home.

Chapter 11
My Wedding Day

We decided to get married right away. We wanted to have a simple wedding: no bridesmaids, no groomsmen, no relatives or guests. No preparations needed to be made. We set the date within a month.

Those were happy days, before my wedding. And yet, every single night I had nightmares when I went to sleep. It was always the same dream: Thornfield Hall lay in ruins; only the outer walls were standing; the roof had crumbled and the windows gaped, black and horrifying like empty sockets in a skull.

The night before my wedding, a feeling of dread woke me up. I did not remember the dream I'd had. It was the middle of the night. I thought about how strange it was that there seemed to be light in the room. It was a dim light, such as a small candle gives out. I thought that Sophie, the maid, had come in. I called out, "Sophie, is that you?" No one answered. I sat up in bed so I could see around me better. My blood turned cold, and it was all I could do not to scream. A tall figure, holding a candle in its hand, was standing by my closet. Its height, its shape, did not remind me of any of the servants. I knew it was a stranger. Slowly, it turned its face to me, stared at me with wild, blazing eyes and started walking toward my bed. I could now see it was a woman. She was wearing a long white gown that looked like a shroud. Her

hair was loose, black, thick and wild—
tangled and matted, as if it had been
soaked in mud or blood that was now
dry. Her face was bloated and had a
black-purple color like a bruise. She
rolled her eyes and grinned, baring long
yellow teeth, then walked past the bed,
to the window. She drew the curtain,
looked out a moment, let the curtain
fall and, turning around toward me
again, blew out the candle. I could no
longer see her in the darkness but I
could hear her footsteps move toward

the door, then out the room and down the long corridor that led to the stairway.

It wasn't a dream, reader. It couldn't have been a dream. In the morning, when I got up, I saw drops of wax on the floor—by the window and in front of the closet. It upset me greatly. When I put my wedding gown on, I looked worried and pale, but I managed to push the incident out of my mind.

It was a beautiful, clear day. We took the carriage to the village church, then walked hand in hand through the churchyard. We had wanted no guests— not even Mrs. Fairfax or Adele—so I expected the church to be totally empty. I was surprised to see two men standing by the last pew. Mr. Rochester was so happy and absorbed that he did not notice them.

I thought nothing of it. They were strangers. I assumed that they entered the church not knowing a wedding was about to take place and decided to stay and watch.

When the service began, the clergyman issued the usual admonition: "I
require and charge you both that if
either of you know any impediment why
ye may not be joined together in matri-
mony, ye do now confess it." He
paused, as is customary, turned his
face toward Mr. Rochester, and opened
his lips to say the next line, "Wilt thou
have this woman for thy wedded
wife?"—when a loud voice from the
back of the church said:

"The marriage must be stopped."

The clergyman stared at the man who
had spoken. Mr. Rochester did not turn
back to look at the man. He seemed to
have recognized the voice. His face had
become bright red.

"Go on with the ceremony," he said to
the priest.

"I cannot," said the clergyman. "Let
the man come forward and explain his
reason for interfering."

"The marriage cannot take place

because Mr. Rochester is already married," the man said. "I am his wife's brother. The gentleman with me is my solicitor. He can show you the marriage deed, and proof that Mrs. Rochester is alive and living in Thornfield Hall, where Mr. Rochester proposes to take his new bride."

"That is impossible," the clergyman said. "I have lived in this village for years and I have never heard of a Mrs. Rochester living at Thornfield Hall."

"She's been locked up like a prisoner in the attic," the solicitor said. "We can produce a witness: Grace Poole, the servant who is paid to be her keeper."

Oh, reader! You can imagine my horror and grief. Suddenly, the crazy laughter, the fire, and the apparition last night in my room made sense. I ran out of the church. Mr. Rochester came after me. Like a wild man, he grabbed me, pushed me into the carriage, and told the driver to take us home.

"You want to see my wife?" he asked. "I'll show you my wife."

I was too horrified to say a word. When we got to Thornfield Hall, he grasped my hand and pulled me after him up the stairs. He knocked savagely at the attic door.

Grace Poole opened up.

"How are you, Mrs. Poole?" he said.

"Tolerably well," Mrs. Poole said.

A blood-curdling scream came from the back of the attic and the woman I had seen in my room rushed at Mr. Rochester with her arms stretched out in front of her, as if she meant to strangle him. Mrs. Poole held her back.

"That is my wife!" Mr. Rochester said.

I ran downstairs, shut myself in my room, and took off my wedding dress. I was too shocked to weep. I was too shocked to feel anything. I changed back to my governess's dress and sat on my bed. What was I to do? I still loved him. I loved him all the more, now that I

understood how he must have suffered all these years, hiding such a terrible secret.

I have to do the right thing, I thought. I have to leave. I cannot stay, because I love him. I'll want to be in his arms. I felt calm and strong, once I had made up my mind. I left my room quietly and went looking for him.

He was in the library. When he saw me, he jumped up from his armchair and walked up to me, looking me in the eyes with despair.

"You must believe me, Jane," he said. "I did not mean to hurt you."

"I know, sir."

"Do you forgive me, Jane?"

There was such love on his face, there was such grief and remorse in his eyes, that I forgave him in my heart, though I could not say the words.

"You think I'm a scoundrel?" he asked.

"Yes, sir."

"Say it then! Say it! Curse me! I deserve it."

"I cannot, sir."

"You still love me, then? You still want to be my wife?"

"You know I cannot be your wife, sir. You have a wife."

"That mad creature?" he said. "You call that mad beast a wife?"

"In the eyes of God, she is. It's not through a fault of her own that she's mad. You shouldn't talk of her with hatred. She can't help what she is or does."

"You know nothing about it," he said.

"I should hate her. I do hate her. She was hateful before she became mad. She was immoral. She was evil."

"You must have known that when you married her, sir."

"I was deceived. I was duped into marrying her. My own father, my own brother deceived me."

He told me then that his father and his brother had conspired to cheat him out of his inheritance. They sent him off to the West Indies to stay with a family friend, who was extremely wealthy and

had a single daughter. They knew that the girl's mother had been mad, and that the girl had inherited her sickness, but they concealed this fact from him and urged him to marry the girl. Once he married her and had use of her large fortune, he would make no claims on Thornfield Hall.

The girl was clever, high-spirited, and extraordinarily beautiful. Some of her odd behavior seemed to be no more than hot temper. Mr. Rochester fell in love with her, and agreed to marry her and

stay in the West Indies as had been his brother and father's wish.

Love blinded him, at first. As soon as the honeymoon was over, however, he realized his mistake.

Gradually, her behavior toward him changed. She started treating him with indifference, then contempt. She had violent outbursts of rage. With time they became so frequent that no servant could tolerate to work in the house. She seemed to like the disarray and filth.

She insulted him in public and used foul language in front of guests.

He was about to start divorce proceedings, when he found out that his mother-in-law, whom he had been led to believe was dead, was, in fact, alive and confined to a mental institution. The doctors told him that his wife suffered from the same mental illness, and it could only get worse. Now he knew he could never divorce her. It would be dishonorable, for his marriage vow had been: "unto sickness and health, as long as I shall live."

He was doomed to live with her forever. He felt such despair.

In the meantime, his father had died. Then, news reached him that his brother had died as well. He could now own Thornfield Hall. He no longer needed to depend on his wife's money.

The idea came to him that he could leave, and go back to England to live. No one would have to know about his wife.

He could take her along, make arrangements that she be taken care of at Thornfield Hall, and he could be free to live his life.

"I did just that," he said. "But I was not free. I knew I was living a lie. I knew I could never be a happy man. I knew I did not have the right to love, to marry. Then, I met you, Jane. I loved you the minute I set eyes on you. I did not show it—I could not show it. I knew I had no right to show it. But my love grew. For the first time in my life I understood what true love is. How could I give that up?"

I looked away from him.

"I know you love me, Jane. Be mine— be mine as you promised."

"I cannot, sir. I must not."

He tried to put his arms around me, but I pushed him away and ran out of the room, afraid that I would give in to him if I stayed one moment longer.

Chapter 12
A New Life

I left at dawn the next day, before anyone had woken up, stealing away like a thief. I took nothing with me but the clothes on my back—the plain dress, which I had worn when I first came to Thornfield Hall. In my haste, I forgot to take my purse. All the money I had on me was the twenty shillings in my pocket.

I was afraid that once they discovered I was missing, they would come after me, so I did not take the road, but walked through the woods and fields. I had no sense of direction and no idea where my wanderings would take me. All I could do was keep going.

It was spring: the fields were covered with flowers; the trees were shining with new leaves, and the birds were singing. Just so, I did not really take in the beauty all around me. I might as well have been marching to my execution. What did I care about my life? I had given up happiness; I had abandoned my true love.

Around noon, I reached a highway. I sat down by the roadside to rest. Soon, I saw a coach approach. I stopped it and asked the coachman how far he'd take me for twenty shillings.

"Whitcross," he said.

I had no idea where Whitcross was, but I asked him to take me there. We rode for several hours. It was dusk when we arrived. Whitcross was no more than

a crossroads. There was a cluster of small houses, a church, and a store. I had expected a large town. I had hoped there would be businesses where I could ask for work. There was nothing. I inquired at the store if anyone in town needed a servant. The woman behind the counter stared at me with suspicion.

"Poor folk live here," she said. "They do their own work."

I did not know what to do. There must be a town near here, I thought. I'll walk on.

I wandered through the fields till it was nightfall and I could barely see. I had not eaten anything all day, and I was weak from hunger. My feet hurt. I had to lie down. But where? I was in an open field, and there was a strong wind. The sky looked as if it might rain. Twice I'd heard thunder, and the air was damp and cold. There was a small wooded hill in the distance, so I decided to try to make my way to it. At least I could find some shelter among the trees.

As I approached, I saw a dim light. It glowed like a star in the mist, but close to the ground. It must be a candle in the window of a house, I thought. It flickered in the darkness, like a dim ray of hope.

As I walked toward it, I could see that the light was, indeed, coming from the window of a house. I hid myself in the shrubbery and looked through a parlor window. An older peasant woman sat by the fire, knitting a sock. Nearby sat two young women about my age, reading a book. By their clothes and their refined faces, I could tell they were ladies.

I knocked at the door. The older woman opened the door and looked at me with the same suspicious expression as the woman at the store.

"Please let me come in," I said. "I have nowhere to go."

"I'll give you a penny," she said. "Now be on your way."

"But I have nowhere to go. I'll die if I sleep out in the rain."

She shut the door on my face.

I turned around and started to move away, when I heard footsteps behind me. I was terrified. A man approached.

"All men must die, and meet their Maker," he said. "But no person in want shall be turned away from my home."

I saw that he had on clergyman's clothes. He placed his hand on my elbow and led me back to the door.

I was given shelter for the night. The next morning I woke up with a high fever. The clergyman said I could stay till I got well. He introduced himself as St. John Rivers and informed me that the two ladies I had seen the night before were his sisters, Diana and Mary. He asked me no questions about myself.

I was sick for over a week. Diana and Mary nursed me back to health, with tenderness and care. They were intelligent, educated women and, sick as I

was, I enjoyed their company greatly. I could tell they were enjoying mine. Their house was too isolated in the woods, and it wasn't often that they had guests.

When, at last, I felt well enough to be on my feet, I got up and put on my dress. They had washed, ironed and mended it where the hem had been torn by my long walk through the fields. Their kindness brought tears to my eyes.

I went down to the drawing room, where they were all gathered.

"I don't know how I could ever repay you," I said. "Let me be a servant."

"You're not a servant," Diana said. "I can see by your hands you've never done a servant's work. Who are you?"

"I am an orphan. I have no relatives, no home. I spent ten years in school, where I was educated to be a teacher. I was a governess for a few months, but I had to leave my place of employment. I cannot tell you why."

"What is your name?" Mr. Rivers asked.

"Jane . . . Elliott," I said. "I cannot give you my real name. I am in hiding. Believe me, sir, I have done no wrong— nothing I should be ashamed of. I appreciate your hospitality and your sisters' compassion, and I am deeply grateful for it, but I refuse to be treated any longer as an object of charity. I'm well capable of work: I can sew, I can do housework—"

"Nonsense," Diana said. "We do not need a servant."

"There's nothing to repay us for," Mary said. "Diana and I have worked as governesses, as well. You're like a friend to us."

"Miss . . . Elliott. I understand that you wouldn't want to be financially dependent on us. I will be on the look-out for employment opportunities for you. In the meantime, you can stay here as one of the family."

And so I did. If Mr. Rivers ever did look for a job for me, I cannot say. The subject was never brought up again. He was a deeply devout man, and I'm sure he believed that he was doing his Christian duty in taking me in. He was sincere, but cold and reserved, acting out of principle rather than true compassion, which comes from the heart. His sisters felt real love for me, however. They wanted me to live with them, and never made me feel that, in having me stay, they were doing a good deed.

My life with them was peaceful. We gardened, took long walks in the woods, did light household chores, and in the evening read quietly by the fire. I had no complaints about my life, but I was unhappy. At night, as I lay down to sleep, I felt lonelier than I had ever felt in my whole lonely life. I thought of Mr. Rochester and how unhappy he must have been. Does he know I still love him? I thought. Does he know that it felt like death to leave him? Does he know it was a sacrifice—of all the happiness I had ever felt, or hoped to have?

Reader, I tried to forget him. But not a moment went by that I did not long to be with him.

One night, I stayed up late. Diana and Mary had gone to bed. Mr. Rivers was preparing his sermon, and I was reading a book. Suddenly, a shiver ran down my spine. I heard a voice cry, "Jane! Jane! Jane!"

"Did you hear that?" I asked Mr. Rivers.

"What?" he asked.

"Jane! Jane!" the voice called out again. It was Mr. Rochester's voice, and it was filled with pain and despair.

I jumped to my feet. "Where are you?" I said. "Where are you?"

There was no answer. I flew to the door and looked out. There was no one in the hall. I ran out to the garden. I saw no one. The moon and stars were covered with black clouds, and a fierce wind hissed through the trees. Patches of fog rose from the ground like shapeless ghosts. I heard my name being called again. I must go to him, I thought. I must leave at once.

But I had to wait till morning, when the coach passed through Witcross. I did not sleep all night. The journey took thirty-six hours. I did not stop on the way to eat or sleep. When I arrived at the village near Thornfield Hall, where the coachman let me off, I was so tired and weak, I could barely stand and yet I found the strength to walk the two miles to the house. I reached the gates and almost fainted, not from exhaustion, but from horror.

Thornfield Hall was a burnt-out shell. There was no roof. The windows had no panes. The front door was charred. A lone figure was sitting on the stoop. As I approached, I could see it was a man. He was wearing no hat and his hair was singed, standing up in tangled tufts. His face was blistered and swollen. His eyes were wide open, but there was no light in them. He stared without blinking.

As he heard my footsteps, he called out: "Is someone there?"

I recognized his voice. But it was not Mr. Rochester I saw in front of me. It was a blind, broken man.

"My dear master," I said. "I'm Jane Eyre. I've come back."

"Am I dreaming?" he said. "Jane Eyre! My Jane?"

"Touch me, sir. Feel my face."

He took me in his arms. He kissed my hair, my face. His lips were trembling, and he was sobbing.

"I've come back to stay," I said.

"Stay! In this ruined place, with a ruined man?"

"The place can be rebuilt, sir. And you'll mend."

"I'll never get my sight back."

"I'll be your eyes, sir. I'll lead you by the hand. I'll describe to you everything I see. I'll never leave your side."

"Do I look hideous, Jane?"

"Yes, sir. But you always did."

"You're mean," he said, smiling. "But you always were."

When I saw his smile I knew he would

let me take care of him. I had been afraid his pride might stand in the way.

"Was anyone killed?" I said.

"No one," he said. "No one—except my wife. I ran up to the attic to save her, but when she saw me coming, she jumped to her death."

I did not want to ask, but I felt sure she must have set the fire.

"Is the house still livable, sir? Is anyone still living here?"

"The back of the house is intact," he said. "Adele is away at school, but all the servants and Mrs. Fairfax are here."

"Let's go in and have supper, sir."

"Edward," he said.

"Let's go in, Edward."

Hand in hand, we walked inside.

Reader, I married him. Surely no woman has ever had a happier marriage. Thornfield Hall was rebuilt. In time, my husband regained sight in one eye. When our first child was born, he could see that the little boy had inherited his features. "A hideous face like mine," he said, smiling with delight. "A handsome man he'll be," I replied.

The End

The End

ABOUT THE AUTHOR

CHARLOTTE BRONTË was born on April 21, 1816, in Yorkshire, England. When her mother and two older sisters died, Charlotte, two remaining sisters, and a brother were cared for by their clergyman father and an aunt. Often left on their own, the children made up stories to entertain one another.

In 1831, Charlotte was sent away to school; she later worked as a schoolteacher and governess. She also tried to open a school of her own, but failed.

Charlotte and her sisters Emily and Anne Brontë all wrote poetry and novels. At first, they used pen names; Charlotte's was Currer Bell. Her first novel, *The Professor*, was rejected by publishers, but *Jane Eyre*, published in 1847, was a great success. Charlotte Brontë wrote several other books before her death on March 31, 1855, but none was ever as popular as *Jane Eyre*.

The Young Collector's Illustrated Classics

The Adventures of Huckleberry Finn
The Adventures of Robin Hood
The Adventures of Sherlock Holmes
The Adventures of Tom Sawyer
Anne of Green Gables
Black Beauty
Call of the Wild
Dracula
Frankenstein
Gulliver's Travels
Heidi
The Hunchback of Notre Dame
Jane Eyre
The Legend of Sleepy Hollow & Rip Van Winkle
A Little Princess
Little Women
Moby Dick
Oliver Twist
Peter Pan
The Prince and the Pauper
Rebecca of Sunnybrook Farm
The Red Badge of Courage
Robinson Crusoe
The Secret Garden
The Strange Case of Dr. Jekyll and Mr. Hyde
Swiss Family Robinson
Tales of Terror and Suspense
The Time Machine
Treasure Island
20,000 Leagues Under the Sea
The War of the Worlds
White Fang

These Illustrated Classics are available for special
and educational sales from:
www.kidsbooks.com

Kidsbooks, Inc.
230 Fifth Avenue
New York, NY 10001
(212) 685-4444